THIS WALKER BOOK
TO:

First published 1986 by Walker Books Ltd
87 Vauxhall Walk, London SE11 5HJ

This edition published 1995

This book has been typeset in New Baskerville Educational.

Printed in Hong Kong

British Library Cataloguing in Publication Data
A catalogue record for this book is available
from the British Library.

ISBN 0-7445-3795-9 (hb)
ISBN 0-7445-3614-6 (pb)

TELL US A STORY

Allan Ahlberg
illustrated by
Colin McNaughton

WALKER BOOKS
AND SUBSIDIARIES
LONDON • BOSTON • SYDNEY

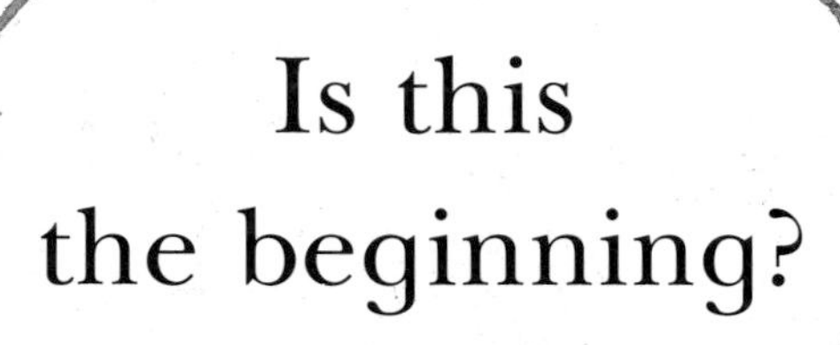
Is this
the beginning?

Contents
The Pig
The Cat
The Horse
The Cow

The Pig

Two little boys
climbed up to bed.

"Tell us a story, Dad,"
they said.

“Right!” said Dad.
“There was once a pig
who ate too much
and got so big
he couldn’t sit down,
he couldn’t bend…

So he ate standing up
and got bigger – The End!"

The Cat

"That story's no good, Dad,"
the little boys said.
"Tell us a better one instead."

"Right!" said Dad.
"There was once a cat
who ate too much
and got so fat

he split his fur
which he had to mend
with a sewing machine
and a zip – The End!”

The Horse

"That story's too mad, Dad,"
the little boys said.

"Tell us another one instead."

“Right!” said Dad.
“There was once a horse
who ate too much
and died, of course –

The End."

The Cow

"That story's too sad, Dad,"
the little boys said.
"Tell us a happier one instead."

"Right..." said Dad.
"There was once a cow
who ate so much
that even now

she fills two fields

and blocks a road,

and when they milk her
she has to be towed!

She wins gold cups
and medals too,
for the creamiest milk
and the *loudest* moo!

Now that's the end,"
said Dad. "No more."
And he shut his eyes
and began to snore.

Then the two little boys
climbed out of bed
and crept downstairs...

to their Mum instead.

The End

Is that *really*
the end?

YES!

MORE WALKER PAPERBACKS
For You to Enjoy

Also by Allan Ahlberg and Colin McNaughton

RED NOSE READERS

Red Nose Readers are the easiest of easy readers - and the funniest!
Red for single words and phrases; yellow for simple sentences;
blue for memorable rhymes.

"Wonderful ... it is hard to imagine better first reading books."
The Times Educational Supplement

"The learning to read process has never been more enjoyable."
Books for Your Children

RED BOOKS

0-7445-1015-5 Bear's Birthday
0-7445-1021-X Big Bad Pig
0-7445-1499-1 Fee Fi Fo Fum
0-7445-1498-3 Happy Worm
0-7445-1496-7 Help!
0-7445-1497-5 Jumping
0-7445-1014-7 Make a Face
0-7445-1016-3 So Can I

YELLOW BOOKS

0-7445-1700-1 Crash! Bang! Wallop!
0-7445-1701-X Me and My Friend
0-7445-1020-1 Push the Dog
0-7445-1019-8 Shirley's Shops

BLUE BOOKS

0-7445-1703-6 Blow Me Down!
0-7445-1018-X One, Two, Flea!
0-7445-1702-8 Look Out for the Seals!

£2.25 each

Walker Paperbacks are available from most booksellers, or by post from B.B.C.S., P.O. Box 941, Hull, North Humberside HU1 3YQ

24 hour telephone credit card line 01482 224626

To order, send: Title, author, ISBN number and price for each book ordered, your full name and address, cheque or postal order payable to BBCS for the total amount and allow the following for postage and packing:
UK and BFPO: £1.00 for the first book, and 50p for each additional book to a maximum of £3.50.
Overseas and Eire: £2.00 for the first book, £1.00 for the second and 50p for each additional book.

Prices and availability are subject to change without notice.